# Robert
## Scariest
## Night

## Also by Barbara Seuling

*Oh No, It's Robert*

*Robert and the Attack of the Giant Tarantula*

*Robert and the Snake Escape*

*Robert and the Great Pepperoni*

*Robert and the Sneaker Snobs*

*Robert and the* Instant Millionaire *Show*

*Robert and the Three Wishes*

*Robert and the Hairy Disaster*

# Robert
## and the
## Scariest
## Night

## by Barbara Seuling
## Illustrated by Paul Brewer

**A
LITTLE APPLE
PAPERBACK**

SCHOLASTIC INC.
New York  Toronto  London  Auckland  Sydney
Mexico City  New Delhi  Hong Kong  Buenos Aires

ISBN 0-439-44375-X

12  11  10  9  8  7  6  5  4  3  2 1        2  3  4  5  6  7/0

Printed in the U.S.A.   40
First Scholastic printing, November 2002

To Gina, with deepest affection
—B. S.

For Janice Brookes
—P. B.

# Contents

# Robert
### and the
## Scariest
## Night

# The Scariest Thing

"**W**ouldn't it be the scariest thing if you were locked inside with the mummies after the museum closed?" asked Emily Asher.

The class was on the bus ride home from their class trip to the Egypt exhibit at the museum.

Robert loved the mummies, but he shuddered. "That would be pretty scary," he agreed.

"The scariest thing for me was the time the lights went out in a storm," Andy Liskin

said. "My mom sent me down to the base-ment for a box of candles. It was dark, and something ran by me. I thought it was a rat, but it was Puffball, our cat. She had fol-lowed me down the stairs."

"Oooooh." Vanessa Nicolini shivered at the thought. "I'd rather stay upstairs in the dark," she said.

"Not me," said Paul Felcher, Robert's best friend. "The dark creeps me out. I always think there are things hiding in the shadows."

"Me, too," said Abby Ranko.

"I was watching a movie on TV once," added Vanessa. "It was really creepy. Just when the scariest part came on, my cat jumped onto me from the bookcase. I didn't stop screaming until my mom threw cold water at my face."

Robert said, "My scariest time was when my brother, Charlie, hid in my closet and popped out to surprise me when I opened the door."

"You're all chickenhearted," said Matt Blakey. "I wouldn't be scared by any of those things."

"Yes, you would," said Andy.

"No, I wouldn't," said Matt. "I'm not a scaredy-cat."

"You should meet my dad," said Robert. "He can scare anyone."

"He can't scare me," Matt answered.

"Don't bet on it," said Paul. "You don't know Robert's dad."

Paul was telling the truth. He was at Robert's house often enough to know. Robert's dad was pretty normal most of the time, but just before Halloween, he changed.

He took out his horror collection. He watched videotapes of his favorite horror movies. He decorated the house with ghoulish delight. He loved getting the house ready for Halloween.

"Your dad sounds cool," said Brian Hoberman.

Robert had never thought of his dad as "cool" before. He had always thought of him as just a regular dad. But he did go ape over Halloween.

"So when do we meet him?" asked Emily.

"My dad?" Robert couldn't believe what he heard.

"Yeah, he sounds great," said Susanne Lee Rodgers. Wow. It took a lot to impress Susanne Lee.

"Well, Halloween is the best time. Come over to my house Saturday and see. I guarantee that he will scare you." Robert looked right at Matt when he said that.

As the bus drove up in front of the school, Susanne Lee, Vanessa, Emily, Abby, Brian, Matt, Andy, and Paul were talking about the Halloween party on Saturday at Robert's house.

# Surprise Party

"A party?" said Robert's mom. "Saturday?" She paced back and forth across the kitchen. Robert's dad was in the living room watching one of his videos. "Robert, you can't invite people to a party without asking me in advance."

"I didn't, exactly," said Robert. "I just said that Dad could scare anyone, and they should come over and see him for themselves around Halloween. The rest just sort of happened."

"What's this?" asked Robert's dad. He had clicked off the video and come into the kitchen.

Robert explained. His dad looked pleased, but Robert's mom was still pacing. "The house is a mess," she said. "I have a bridal shower to go to on Saturday and I won't even be around."

"I will," said Robert's dad.

"Yeah, Mom. Dad and I can do it." Robert thought it would be great to have the party with just his dad home. His dad wasn't as strict about things as his mom.

"Right," said his dad. "What do we have to do?"

"Well," she sputtered. "Cleaning . . . and you'll need party treats and paper goods and . . . and . . . decorations . . . and . . . entertainment . . ."

"We can do all that, Clare," said Robert's dad. "Don't worry." He winked at Robert.

"We'll go shopping together after school tomorrow."

Robert looked at his dad with a big thank-you in his eyes.

Robert's mom gave in. She said she would tidy up the house if they did the rest.

"Let's get the stuff from the basement and see what we've got," said Robert.

Mr. Dorfman was a real movie fan, especially horror movies. He had a collection of costumes, masks, props like fake hands and scars, theatrical makeup, and other stuff. He even had a Dracula cape he once wore to a grown-up party at a horror fans' convention. Every Halloween, the collection came out, and Robert found things he had forgotten about since last year.

Robert's dad went down to the basement and brought up a big cardboard box marked "HORROR." He went back for two more cartons after that.

They opened the cartons in the living room. In one were the rubber masks and hands. Next came the makeup case, the Dracula cape, and various props. In the third box were assorted decorations.

"Look, here's Henry," said Robert. He unfolded a huge skeleton with movable limbs. "Can I hang him?" he asked.

"Sure, Tiger. Go ahead."

Robert opened the front door and hung Henry right next to the door knocker. The hook was still there from last year.

Digging into the box again, Robert pulled out cardboard pictures of horrible creatures. He taped them to the front windows to look like they were peering out.

Next came bloody hands, bloodshot eyeballs, fake guts, bats with flapping wings, phony cobwebs, and various electronic items, like talking boxes and dismembered hands that walked across the table when the batteries were turned on.

Last, but not least, was the Halloween tree. Every year they set it up and hung creepy ornaments on its branches. Robert smiled. Halloween at the Dorfman house had begun.

# Too Late Now

On Friday, Robert was ready when his dad got home from work. He raced outside and jumped into the backseat, hooking his seat belt.

"Can we go to the party store first?" he asked.

"Okay, we'll start there," said his dad.

They bought party games and prizes, decorations, paper plates and cups and napkins, and miscellaneous spooky figures and toys. One was a witch who cackled and whose eyes flashed red when you lifted her up.

Robert felt a little weird. He knew his mom would have made him put half the stuff back by now, but his dad just let him keep adding to the cart.

Next, they went to the Super Shopper. As they stood in line at the checkout, Robert began to worry.

"Dad, is Charlie going to be at my party?"

"Your brother, Charlie, was invited to a party at Barney's house," his dad answered. That was a relief. Charlie could be a real tease and spoil things.

They waited while the clerk rang up three packages of disposable diapers for the person ahead of them.

"What about music, Dad? And entertainment?"

"Got it under control, Tiger. Will you stop worrying? This is going to be fun."

"Dad?"

"Yes, Robert?" The line moved up by one person, and they started putting their bags of candy and jugs of juice drinks on the moving belt.

"Will you tell some of your scary stories? Please?"

"Sure, if you want me to," answered his father. "I think you're worrying too much. You'll have a great party. I have a few surprises in mind guaranteed to send kids screaming." He grinned.

Robert smiled back. What was his dad going to do? Would his friends like being scared or would they think his dad was weird? Halloween was sort of about being scared, so he hoped they would like his dad's surprises. Sometimes they could be

pretty surprising, but that's what was such fun. Would the other kids see it that way? Maybe he should have just gone out trick-or-treating.

The cash register rang out *ching! ching! ching!* It was too late now to change his mind.

# Uncle Albert

**R**obert got out of bed and staggered into the bathroom. He got dressed, fed his birds, Flo and Billie, and said good morning to Fuzzy, his tarantula. She moved her legs slightly, which was her way of saying good morning.

He thumped downstairs, and as he brushed aside the fake cobwebs hanging in the kitchen doorway, he remembered: It was Saturday—the day of the Halloween party.

Last night, he had stayed up late putting up pictures of witches and skulls and black cats. On the coffee table, the crystal polar bear had been replaced by the plastic witch with the glowing eyes. Robert lifted it up to hear the witchy voice cackle.

His dad must have stayed up really late. He had hung the cobwebs and draped all the furniture with black crepe paper streamers. The Halloween tree stood on the dining room table, all assembled with bats and worms and spiders hanging from its branches.

Robert sat at the table and poured Crispy Crunchy Flakes into a bowl. He reached for the milk container and poured. It was green.

"Mo—o—m . . ."

"It's your father, dear." His mom sighed. "He put food dye in the milk. It's harmless."

He should have known. Robert smiled. "Where is Dad?" he asked, spooning in some of the cereal.

"In the living room. But finish your breakfast first."

Robert gulped down his cereal and washed it down with orange juice.

He found his father stuffing an old plaid flannel shirt and a pair of jeans with newspapers.

"What are you doing?" Robert asked.

"Getting Uncle Albert ready," said his father. He lifted the stuffed clothing onto the easy chair in the corner. Robert watched as his dad tucked the shirt part into the pants part. Then he stuffed socks with more newspaper, stuck them inside a pair of his shoes, and added these to the rest of the figure in the chair. Without the head and hands, it looked something like a scarecrow, but a lot scarier.

Robert's dad picked up an over-the-head rubber mask of a bald guy with bushy eyebrows and a deep frown on his face. The lower lip hung a little. The face was wickedly ugly. Robert's dad stuffed more newspaper inside the mask.

"Here, help me with this, Tiger," he said. Robert opened the neck of Uncle Albert's shirt while his dad put the mask in place. Where the neck of the mask met the shirt, his dad tied a scarf around and knotted it.

"What about his hands?" asked Robert.

"I'm glad you asked," said his dad. He lifted up two big hollow rubber hands, all gnarled and hairy. He arranged them so they stuck out of the shirt cuffs. Uncle Albert looked natural and relaxed, his hands resting on the arms of the chair and his legs crossed. It was perfect.

As Mrs. Dorfman walked through the living room, she did a double take. "Oh,

my," she said. "He looks so real, sitting there."

"That's the point," said Mr. Dorfman. Robert saw that his dad was having fun.

"I can't wait for the kids to see Uncle Albert," said Robert.

"Do you think Matt Blakey will like it?" his dad asked.

"I'm sure he'll like it," Robert said, "but I don't know if it will scare him. He says he's not scared of anything."

"Ah, a challenge," said his dad. His eyes gleamed. "I love challenges."

"How are you going to scare him?" Robert knew his dad well enough to know he'd been thinking up ideas.

"You'll have to wait to find out, Tiger. I can't spoil all the surprises for you. You already know about Uncle Albert."

# Wel-l-l-l-come!

**R**obert decided to get into his costume so his mom could see him before she left for the bridal shower. His dad let him use the Dracula cape, and his mom helped him put on the theatrical makeup—green on his skin, black around his eyes, dark shadows on his cheeks to make them look sunken, and bright red lips. A set of vampire teeth made it perfect.

"You're the best vampire I've ever seen," she told him. Having his mom around, Robert felt everything was going to be okay. When

Robert saw her blue Toyota leave the driveway a few minutes later, he felt a little less certain.

The doorbell rang around five o'clock. Robert leaped from the sofa and ran to the door. Emily came in first, in a witch costume with a tall, pointy hat. Brian followed her as a Martian.

"Wel-l-l-l-come," Robert the Vampire said. He held his hands high and clawlike, spreading open the cape.

Mr. Dorfman, in his over-the-head werewolf mask and a pair of hairy hands, pointed the way into the living room. The children saw Uncle Albert and stopped short.

"Come right in," said Mr. Dorfman. "This is Uncle Albert. He doesn't say much. He just likes to—observe." Emily and Brian hung back.

Next came Vanessa as a ballerina, Matt as a mad doctor in a white lab coat with red stains all over it, and Paul in a clown suit with a big red rubber nose.

"Meet Uncle Albert," said Robert's dad to the new group. "He's not very sociable." The kids stared, but only Matt moved closer. He went up to the dummy's face and looked into its eyes. Vanessa squealed. When Matt was convinced it was just a dummy, he moved away from Uncle Albert and into the dining room. The table had been set up with the Halloween tree and bowls filled with miniature candy bars, orange and black jelly beans, marshmallow ghosts and black licorice cats, candy pumpkins and candy corn.

"Help yourselves," said Robert. He tried not to sound too cheerful. After all, he was a vampire. He grabbed a handful of black and orange jelly beans for himself. Matt left to take another look at Uncle Albert. This time he poked a finger into Uncle Albert's chest. After a little more poking, he left the dummy alone.

More kids arrived. Susanne Lee came as the Statue of Liberty, Abby as a cat, and Andy as a mummy, with toilet paper bandages wound around him and trailing behind. Robert introduced them to Uncle Albert. Susanne Lee walked right up to him and said, "Oh, hello, Uncle Albert." When she turned around, she jumped. Mr. Dorfman's werewolf mask got her. Robert had to laugh.

Robert's dad kept the music playing. Sometimes he played eerie background music from horror movies, and sometimes

the sound of witches cackling, creaky
doors, and winds howling. Robert recog-
nized these from a special-effects CD that
his dad owned.

Matt still looked suspiciously at Uncle Albert. Finally, he joined the rest of the kids as they were getting ready to bob for apples in the kitchen. Matt was plenty curious, but he didn't seem the least bit scared.

# Eyeballs and Worms

Robert's dad, no longer in his werewolf mask, had a huge covered pot in his arms. "Who's hungry?" he called.

"What is it? What is it?" the children cried.

"My own special stew," said Mr. Dorfman with a devilish grin. "I need someone—a brave soul—who will put his hand into this stew of mine and stir it around."

"No way," said Brian.

"Uh-uh, not me," said Paul. The boys laughed nervously, but nobody moved.

The girls all stayed frozen in a huddle.

"Ah," said Mr. Dorfman. "Is everyone afraid, then?" He turned to Matt. "You, Matt. Are you afraid?"

Matt stepped forward. "I . . . I'm not afraid. What's in there?" he asked.

Mr. Dorfman blindfolded Matt. "Only eyeballs and worms," he said. "It won't harm you."

"Eee-yew!" said Abby, backing away. Emily hid behind her. Robert smiled. He knew it was just peeled grapes and cold spaghetti, but he didn't tell. Mr. Dorfman took the lid off the pot and guided Matt's hand to the edge of it.

"Reach in, real deep," said Mr. Dorfman. Matt put his hand farther into the pot. "Yuck!" he said, making a horrible face.

"Now fish around until you find a card. Pull it out and read it. You have to do whatever it says."

Matt pulled his hand out, waving a card. He removed his blindfold.

"What does it say?" asked Paul.

Matt read, "Hop around the room on one foot while crowing COCK-A-DOODLE-DOO."

As the children watched, Matt started hopping and crowing. Giggles and howls filled the room.

"I'll go next," said Susanne Lee. She did, and everyone watched for signs that she was getting grossed out. She was fine. Her card read, recite "Mary Had a Little Lamb" backward. Paul went next. He had to do a somersault.

The games continued for a while. They were playing pin the tail on the black cat when the doorbell rang. It was the pizza delivery guy.

Mr. Dorfman invited the children into the dining room. He put two pizza boxes on the table. Brian eagerly opened the first box and yelled in surprise. It was rubber snakes. The second box revealed a bloody finger, fake guts, bloodshot eyeballs, a dismembered ear, and a piece of brain.

"Eee-yew!" cried Vanessa, but she giggled.

"Gross," said Emily, in spite of the smile on her face.

Mr. Dorfman exchanged the two boxes of horrible things for two other boxes, this time real pizza. "Help yourselves," he said, and they all dove for a piece.

# Scary Stories

**R**obert had just bitten into a piece of pepperoni pizza when his dad walked back in. "Would you like me to tell a scary story?" he asked.

"Yes!" they all cried.

He turned out the lights, lit a single candle that cast weird shadows on his face, and began to spin a spooky tale.

It was about creaks in the floor and a corpse rising from the grave and bodies buried in the walls of a house. The children were spellbound. When Mr. Dorfman

finished one story, they asked for another.
He told a gruesome story about a floating
head that came bobbing down the stairs at
night, its eyes aglow.

With each addition of something more horrid or loathsome, there were groans and gasps and whimpers.

As the story ended, the candle went out, and they were in the dark. Robert had seen his dad do this before. He kept very quiet. Without warning, Mr. Dorfman let out a scream, and they heard and felt a thud. The children jumped up, screaming, in the dark. Mrs. Dorfman came running in, still in her coat, and turned on the light.

"Mom," said Robert. "You're home."

Mr. Dorfman was stretched out on the floor. He opened his eyes. "Hello, Clare," he said.

"I think maybe that's enough fright for one Halloween night," she said.

"Oh, please, Mrs. Dorfman. We won't scream anymore. Honest." The children begged for more, but Mrs. Dorfman was firm.

"Maybe next year," Mr. Dorfman told them. He winked.

"It's time for cake," said Mrs. Dorfman. "Take your places at the table." The children went back to their seats.

As they dug their plastic forks into the cake, frosted in orange icing, Mrs. Dorfman poured a cherry-colored fruit drink into their paper cups.

Robert went up to his father. "Dad, you haven't scared Matt Blakey," he whispered with some urgency.

Mr. Dorfman frowned. "I know. You were right. He's a really tough case."

# Gotcha!

"**R**obert, why don't you take your friends up to your room to see your tarantula?" said Robert's mom.

Robert stared at his mom. Sometimes she could surprise him. She had never showed any interest in his tarantula before.

"Okay," he said. "Follow me."

"You have a tarantula?" said Brian, his eyes wide.

"That's a spider, right?" asked Emily in a shaky voice.

"Yes, a huge spider," said Robert, hoping that would scare Matt a little.

Upstairs in his room, Robert introduced them to Fuzzy. He told them how he got her when Susanne Lee brought her over one day because her cat wanted to eat Fuzzy.

"Everybody knows Robert loves animals," Susanne Lee said. "He seemed like the right person to adopt Fuzzy."

Robert did not add that Susanne Lee had practically forced the tarantula on him. Or how scared he was to sleep in the same room with Fuzzy at first.

After the children saw Fuzzy and Robert's doves, Flo and Billie, they went back downstairs. Mrs. Dorfman reminded them that it was almost eight o'clock, so they should begin to gather their belongings. "Your parents will be here soon," she said.

They sat around the living room, clutching their bags of treats. They no longer paid attention to the figure in the easy chair, except for Matt. He went over and reached out to touch Uncle Albert's sleeve. Suddenly, the figure grabbed him. Matt let out a scream so loud the rest of the children

started screaming as well. Mrs. Dorfman came running. Vanessa was hiccuping between screams. Abby ran for the bathroom and locked herself in.

Mrs. Dorfman went over to Matt and put her arm around his shoulders. "It's only a trick," she said, comforting him. Uncle Albert stood up. The children were transfixed. Matt clung to Mrs. Dorfman.

Meanwhile, Robert talked to Abby through the bathroom door to convince her it was okay to come out. "It was only a trick, Abby. Come on, you'll see." Abby came out, but she stayed very close to Robert.

"This is our neighbor, Tom," said Mr. Dorfman, pointing to Uncle Albert. "He agreed to come over to help with the surprise." Tom took off the hands and the Uncle Albert mask.

"Hi," he said.

"You . . . you were in there . . . the . . . the . . . whole time?" Matt stammered.

"No," said Mr. Dorfman, "While you were upstairs, Tom made the switch, getting into Uncle Albert's clothes. I put the mask and rubber hands on him and got him into the same position the dummy had been in."

"Robert, you were right," said Susanne Lee. "Your dad is fun."

"Yeah," said Matt. "This was a great party."

"Thanks," said Robert, catching his dad's eye.

As parents arrived and thanked the Dorfmans, Robert overheard some of the conversations.

"It was great!" Brian told his mom.

Susanne Lee told her mom the scary stuff was "awesome."

Vanessa told her dad the best part was listening to scary stories by candlelight.

When Matt's dad picked him up, he said to Matt, "So, did you have a good time?"

Matt nodded. "Dad, I was so scared I jumped ten feet!" They went off toward their car, Matt chattering away.

In the house, Robert looked at his dad. His dad looked at him. As they closed the door behind them, they gave each other a high five.

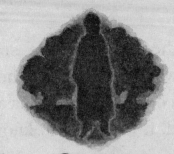

# The Stranger

Everyone but Paul had been picked up. He was staying overnight with Robert. They were tired but a little wound up, so the two boys lounged on the sofa while Mr. Dorfman tidied up the living room around them. Robert picked up the plastic witch and listened to her cackle. Her eyes glowed on and off. He and Paul giggled.

In the dining room, Mrs. Dorfman was clearing off the table, dumping paper plates and used napkins and forks into a big black trash bag. Robert was glad his mom was home in time for some of the party, anyway. Even though she didn't let them carry on with their tricks as much as his dad did, it felt good to know she was there.

Paul got up to help clear the table with Mrs. Dorfman. Robert followed.

"Well, thank you," said Mrs. Dorfman. "I never had a vampire and a clown help me with the cleanup before." They smiled, too tired to answer.

At last, they said good night and climbed the stairs to Robert's room. They got out of their costumes and scrubbed off the makeup.

"Don't you wish sometimes you could be as surprised as everyone else by your dad?" asked Paul.

Robert thought about it. "No, it's okay. I kind of like being in on the jokes and watching other people see them for the first time."

"Did you know about Uncle Albert and Tom?"

"I suspected it, but I didn't know for sure until my mom sent us upstairs. I knew they needed us out of the way for something, and that was probably it."

As they got into bed, they heard a noise out back, in the yard. Robert got up and went to the window. He motioned for Paul to come, too.

Paul gasped when he looked down. Below the window was an ugly stranger in a trench coat. The stranger stared up at them.

"See what I mean?" said Robert. "That's my dad again. That's another mask he's wearing. We'll pretend to be scared, but I know it's him."

Robert pretended to scream and threw his hands up in the air. Paul followed him and did the same, jumping around like he was really frightened. While they were at the window, acting scared, there was a knock on Robert's door.

Robert went to the door and opened it. There stood his dad.

"AAAAAAAH!" Robert screamed. Paul screamed. Robert ran to the window. The stranger was still in the yard, so it couldn't be his dad!

"Dad! Look!" Robert went back to his dad and pulled him to the window by his sleeve.

Mr. Dorfman looked out the window.

"See him?" Robert asked.

Mr. Dorfman nodded. "I'll go down and see who it is," he said. "You stay here."

Robert and Paul watched nervously from the window as Mr. Dorfman appeared in the yard and approached the stranger. The stranger held up his fists as if he wanted to fight.

"Look out, Dad!" Robert called.

Both men looked up at the window—and waved, as Tom, the neighbor, pulled off his rubber mask.

"Oh, no!" said Robert.

"They got us!" said Paul.

"Yeah," said Robert. "He even fooled me." His dad really *was* cool.

The boys fell back into bed, collapsing in laughter.

"Paul?" said Robert, after they turned out the light.

"Yeah?"

"Next year I'm going to have a party and invite the whole class."

"But your mom said you can't invite kids over for a party without asking her."

"No, she said I can't invite people to a party without asking her *in advance,*" said Robert. "This time I'm asking her a whole year in advance."

He pulled the covers up over his head and went to sleep.

**BARBARA SEULING** is a well-known author of fiction and nonfiction books for children, including several books about Robert. She divides her time between New York City and Vermont.

**PAUL BREWER** likes to draw gross, silly situations, which is why he enjoys working on books about Robert so much. He lives in San Diego, California, with his wife and two daughters.